Baby Ant Has Stinky Pants

Written by **Sigmund Brouwer**

Illustrated by **Sharon Dahl**

Created by **Don Sullivan**

Thomas Nelson, Inc.
Nashville

Published in Nashville, Tennessee, by Tommy Nelson®,
a division of Thomas Nelson, Inc.

Scripture quotations used in this book are from the Holy Bible,
New Century Version, copyright © 1987, 1988, 1991 by Word Publishing,
Nashville, Tennessee. Used by permission.

Library of Congress Cataloging-in-Publication Data
Brouwer, Sigmund, 1959-
    Baby Ant has stinky pants / written by Sigmund Brouwer ; illustrated
by Sharon Dahl ; created by Don Sullivan
       p. cm.—(Bug's-eye view books)
    Summary: Baby Ant's stinky pants create problems in the Ant family.
  ISBN 0-8499-7731-2
    [1. Ants—Fiction.] I. Dahl, Sharon, ill. II. Sullivan, Don, 1953-
III. Title. IV. Series.

PZ7.B79984 Bab 2001
[E]—dc21   2001034519

Printed in Italy
01 02 03 04 05 PBI 5 4 3 2 1

The Bible Says . . .

Do not be lazy, but work hard . . .

—Romans 12:11a

Baby Ant had stinky pants.

Baby Ant had stinky pants
really bad.

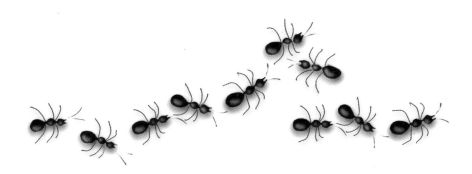

"Who will change Baby Ant's
stinky pants?" asked Mommy Ant.

"I can't change Baby Ant's stinky pants," Annie Ant called out. "My chore is to make lunch."

"I can't change Baby Ant's stinky pants," Arnie Ant called out. "My chore is to wash the dishes."

"I can't change Baby Ant's stinky pants," Daddy Ant called out. "My chore is to take out the trash."

So Mommy Ant changed Baby Ant's
stinky pants. Mommy Ant gave
Baby Ant's stinky pants to
Daddy Ant to throw out
with the trash.

The trash can was still full,
so Daddy Ant hid Baby Ant's
stinky pants. Daddy Ant had
other things to do. He would
throw out Baby Ant's stinky
pants later.

The sink still had too
many dishes, so Arnie Ant
hid the pot. Arnie Ant had
other things to do. He
would clean the pot later.

Lunch was still not made.
Annie Ant saw a pot in the oven.
"Good," she said, "Mommy Ant did
my chore." Annie Ant had other
things to do. She would check
on lunch later.

Next time Baby Ant had
stinky pants, everyone
did their chores. Right away.

Let's Talk About . . .

What kinds of chores need to
be done at your house?

Why should you help your family?

How can you be responsible at
school, work, and church?

What can you do to show
others how to be helpful?

Lord our God, be pleased with us.
Give us success in what we do.

—Psalm 90:17